Helena Pielichaty (pronounced Pierre-li-hatty) has written numerous books for children, including *Simone's Letters*, which was nominated for the Carnegie Medal. Football has often been a theme in Helena's writing, beginning with *There's Only One Danny Ogle* (OUP 2000) about a boy who happens to support Helena's favourite club, Huddersfield Town. Helena is a fan of the women's game, too, influenced no doubt by her Auntie Pat playing for Yorkshire Copperworks in the 1950s. Her daughter also played for various teams from the age of 10 onwards. The Griffins U11s, a local girls' team, inspired many of the stories in Girls FC.

Are All Brothers Foul?

Helena Pielichaty

WALKER
BOOKS

To Phil Hugan for all his time and invaluable help

First published 2009 by Walker Books Ltd
This edition published 2018
87 Vauxhall Walk, London SE11 5HJ

10 9 8 7 6 5 4 3 2 1

Text © 2009 Helena Pielichaty
Cover illustration © 2018 Eglantine Ceulemans

The right of Helena Pielichaty to be identified as author of this work has been asserted by her in accordance with the Copyright, Designs and Patents Act 1988

This book has been typeset in Helvetica and Handwriter

Printed and bound in Great Britain by CPI Group (UK) Ltd

British Library Cataloguing in Publication Data:
a catalogue record for this book is available from the British Library

ISBN 978-1-4063-8349-2

www.walker.co.uk

MIX
Paper from
responsible sources
FSC® C020471
www.fsc.org
FSC

The Team

⚽ **Megan "Meggo" Fawcett** GOAL

⚽ **Petra "Wardy" Ward** DEFENCE

⚽ **Lucy "Goose" Skidmore** DEFENCE

⚽ **Dylan "Dyl" or "Psycho 1" McNeil** LEFT WING

⚽ **Holly "Hols" or "Wonder" Woolcock** DEFENCE

⚽ **Veronika "Nika" Kozak** MIDFIELD

⚽ **Jenny-Jane "JJ" or "Hoggy" Bayliss** MIDFIELD

⚽ **Gemma "Hursty" or "Mod" Hurst** MIDFIELD

⚽ **Eve "Akka" Akboh** STRIKER

⚽ **Tabinda "Tabby" or "Tabs" Shah** STRIKER/MIDFIELD

⚽ **Daisy "Dayz" or "Psycho 2" McNeil** RIGHT WING

⚽ **Amy "Minto" or "Lil Posh" Minter** VARIOUS

Official name: Parrs Under 11s, also known as the Parsnips

Ground: Lornton FC, Low Road, Lornton

Capacity: 500

Affiliated to: the Nettle Honeyball Women's League junior division

Sponsors: Sweet Peas Garden Centre, Mowborough

Club colours: red and white; red shirts with white sleeves, white shorts, red socks with white trim

Coach: Hannah Preston

Assistant coach: Katie Regan

Pre-match Interview

Hi! My name is Lucy Skidmore and I play in defence for the Parrs Under 11s. Megan has given me the task of carrying straight on from where Petra left off. Well, not straight on, as it was the summer holidays and we didn't have any more matches or practices for a few weeks, and I'm guessing Megan doesn't want me to tell you that Holly went to Disneyland Florida, or that Nika went back to see her grandparents in the Ukraine, or that I didn't have a holiday because everything was a bit upside-down with Dad moving out.

Anyway, my target is to tell you about the start of our first season in the Nettie Honeyball League. Yes, the Nettie Honeyball League! I bet you can guess how excited we all were. This was the real deal, with fixture lists and home and away matches and cup runs and league tables.

Bring it on!

Truly yours,
Lucy

P.S. I've included a copy of the fixture list (see next page) to show the matches I cover. You can fill in the results after you've read each match report if you like!

The Nettie Honeyball Women's Football League junior division

Parrs U11s (Parsnips) Fixture List

Week	Date	Opposition	H/A	Kick-off	Result
1	Sat 1 Sept	Cuddlethorpe Tigers (friendly)	A	10.30	
2	Sat 8 Sept	Grove Belles	H	11.00	
3	Sat 15 Sept	Hixton Lees Juniors	H	10.30	
4	Thurs 20 Sept	Southfields Athletic	A	18.00	
5	Sun 23 Sept	Cuddlethorpe Tigers	H	11.00	
6		No match			
7	Sat 6 Oct	Tembridge Vixens	A	10.30	

☆ All teams will play seven-a-side

☆ All matches will be sixty minutes in duration with ten-minutes for half-time

☆ There is no limit to the number of substitutions (roll on/roll off)

☆ Nettie Honeyball Women's League Code of Conduct applies at all times

☆ MATCH ONE ☆

Pre-season Friendly

Teams:
Parrs U11s (Parsnips) v.
Cuddlethorpe Tigers

Date & venue:
Saturday 1 September
at Cuddlethorpe Playing Fields,
Cuddlethorpe

Kick-off:
10.30

Attendance:
0

Sorry, but I can't write about the first match because it was cancelled. Great start, huh? Hannah and Katie had to phone round everyone on Friday to tell us. She said two Tigers were still on holiday in Ibiza, one had a broken wrist after falling off a water slide in Menorca and one had moved out of the area without letting them know until that morning.

So at half-ten, which should have been kick-off, I opened the door to my dad to start a match-free Saturday. He had just arrived from Bicester, where he now lives, to take my brother, Harry, and me out. Bicester is a hundred and two miles away and over an hour and a half's drive, so he looked tired. A hundred and two miles is a long way to drive to pick your kids up – but Dad can't sleep here now or have meals with us or even watch *Gillette Soccer Saturday*. "It wouldn't be appropriate," was how Mum explained it when I asked why not.

Anyway, we were in the sitting room, waiting for Harry to get ready. Dad was reading the Parrs newsletter Hannah had given to everyone last week after we'd returned to training. Believe it or not, by twenty to eleven he still hadn't got further than the heading! "The Nettie Honeyball League? Who or what on earth is a Nettie Honeyball?" Dad asked.

That's the trouble with having a dad who's a history teacher and pub-quiz captain; he gets distracted by names and places. You do not want to go on a visit to somewhere old like Cambridge or Lincoln with him. It takes three years to get down one street. Mum's a teacher, too, but she teaches PE, so visiting new towns with her isn't such a problem – unless you're in a school minibus and late for a netball match; then she gets well stressed out, I bet.

"I don't know who or what on earth a Nettie

Honeyball is either, Dad," I said. "I just want you to check the dates, please. Can you come to all the matches? Apart from the Thursday night one?"

He didn't answer; he just kept banging on about Nettie Honeyball. "Nettie Honeyball, though. What a fantastic name! That beats some of mine. Did I tell you about that time I taught a girl called Chelsea Bunn?"

"Dad, the dates!"

"Chelsea Bunn! Honestly. Lovely girl, though. Very bright."

"Dad, pleeeeease…"

He winked at me then, to show he was only winding me up. "Of course I can come! When have I ever missed you playing football?"

I let out a huge sigh of relief. So many things were going to be different from now on; it was good to know I could rely on that, at least. "Shall I go and see where Harry is?" I asked.

"Yep. You do that while I google Nettie Honeyball."

But just then Mum, who was supposed to be keeping out of the way until we'd gone, strode into the sitting room, quick as a flash, as if she'd been listening to every word. "Rob, you can't," she told him.

He tensed round the jaw. "Can't what?"

"Google anything. You're going *out*, remember. The deal during term time was that I have the kids *five* days a week, you do the weekends – i.e. *two* days."

"Understood. Though I'd happily swap places and have them the entire *seven* days a week if *you* wanted to go and live and teach in Bicester instead, dearest."

These days Dad says "dearest" to wind Mum up, but she wasn't distracted; she often umpires netball and hockey matches, so she knows how to focus. "*Two* of the seven days; apart from the next two weekends, when it's *one* day because you're spending the Sundays decorating."

"Again, if you want to swap places and do the

decorating while I have the kids, be my guest."

"Oh, very funny."

"I'm glad you think so."

Mum gave Dad a look that said *"Don't start"* and he gave her a look that said *"Give me a break"* and I ran upstairs to find Harry and tell him to get a move on quick.

He was in the bathroom, gelling his hair, just as Dad had predicted. He frowned at me, and when I asked him to hurry he shoved the bathroom door shut, but he was downstairs soon after and the three of us were ready to go.

"See you at teatime." Mum smiled, relaxing now the new rules were working.

"Will you be all right on your own?" I asked her.

She rolled her eyes. "With the amount of planning for school I've got to do? You bet."

"OK," I said and took Dad's hand.

We spent the day in Mowborough. I enjoyed it, mainly because we did what we always did, more or less. We changed our library books, then stopped off at W. H. Smith's and bought a *Guardian* for Dad and a *Match* for me and an *SFX* magazine for Harry.

At lunchtime we tried to get into Pasta Roma, but it was full so we went next door to McDonald's instead. Of course most of Mowborough High, where Dad used to teach and Mum still does teach, hang out there, so every two seconds someone came up to Dad to say "Yay, Mr Skidmore" or "Wotcha, Harry." Harry cringed when a bunch of girls waved and blew kisses at him, and Dad didn't help by teasing. "Bit of a babe magnet are we, son?"

In the afternoon we went to the Odeon and saw the new *X-Men* film, which was wicked. Harry had already seen it mid-week with his friends, but he didn't tell Dad that.

After all that we came home. It felt different then, because instead of driving the car up to the garage we parked on the road. "Shall we listen to the results on the radio first? See if United won?"

I asked. (Dad and me both follow Manchester United.)

"No, I'd best set off. I'll wait until *Match of the Day* tonight."

"OK," I said, and gave him a massive hug. He hugged me back, really tight, and I might have cried but I felt the fixture list crackle in his pocket and that helped because I knew I'd see him again soon. "Love you loads," I said, planting a double whopper of a kiss on his cheek.

"Love you, too, Lucy."

"Don't forget I'll need to be at the ground for ten next week. Can you be here at half-past nine?"

"God and the M40 willing."

From the back seat, I felt Harry tap me on the shoulder. "What time's it finish?"

"Twelve."

"Twelve? Yes! Nice one, sis. That means I get an extra long lie-in. Ta muchly."

Dad twisted round to look at him. "What do you mean?"

"You go do the football thing and pick me up after. Sorted."

"That's not part of the deal I've got with Mum, Harry," Dad said softly. "You've *both* got to be with me to give her a break."

"But I don't want to watch football," Harry said. "I hate football; it's lame."

"Oh, come on, it's only for an hour," Dad said. "We can go to McDonald's straight after."

Harry scowled. "How is setting off at half-nine and finishing at twelve an hour?"

"I'm sorry, Harry," I said, feeling guilty because I hadn't really thought of that – him *having* to come and watch me play because of our new routine.

"This stinks," Harry snarled, and got out of the car.

☆ MATCH TWO ☆

Teams:
Parrs U11s (Parsnips) v.
Grove Belles

Date & venue:
Saturday 8 September
at Lornton FC, Low Road,
Lornton
(home match)

Kick-off:
11.00

Attendance:
29

2

My alarm rang at eight o'clock. I jumped out of bed, had a quick wash and put on my shorts and shirt. I was so excited for this one! At last! The first match of the season! I just couldn't wait. I sat on the edge of the bed to pull on my socks – left foot first every time. It's my ritual. Every decent player has one. After that I checked my boots were clean, dropped them back in my kit bag, threw on my comfy trainers and clattered downstairs for breakfast.

Dad arrived at 9.28. I gave him a cuddle and thanked him for being two minutes early.

"The roads aren't bad this time on a Saturday morning," he said. "Everyone's still in bed."

"Oh."

"Including your brother, no doubt."

"'Scuse me! Brother in the room!" Harry said, suddenly appearing and heading straight for the fridge. He peered inside, grunted, then slammed the door shut again. "What?" he said when he saw us staring. I admit I was surprised he was up and dressed. I think Dad was too. "*What?*" he asked again.

"Nothing," Dad said.

Harry gave a sly grin and patted his back pocket. "Twenty quid's not a bad incentive to get out of bed."

"Your mum actually paid you?" Dad asked in disbelief.

"Bribery and corruption. Works every time," Harry said cheerfully, then strode to the back door. "Come on, then; it's gone half-past. What we waiting for?"

In the car, Harry said I could sit in the front, even though it was his turn. "You two can talk football while I get some kip," he said.

"I'd rather you sat next to me so we can talk

about your little extortion racket," said Dad. He sounded a bit cross.

"Nah, you're all right," Harry replied, sliding into the back without a second's thought.

I waited on the pavement, feeling tense in case it turned into an argument, but Dad just scowled at the bedroom window where Mum's office was, then nodded to me to get into the front seat.

We arrived at the ground at ten to ten. I dived out of the car immediately, keen to get going. Mr Cadogan, my teacher from last year, always used to laugh at me when it was the games lesson, because I'd be changed and doing star jumps while everyone else was still packing away their pencil cases. "Blimey, Lucy; pace yourself, girl! You make me exhausted just watching you!" he'd tell me, but I couldn't help it. Sport. I just love it! As well as playing football for the Parsnips I go to football, netball and athletics practice at school. Athletics had finished now, and netball and football didn't start again at school until next week, so I was doubly excited about playing today.

I took a deep breath and glanced around. The seven-a-side pitch we used was hidden on the other side of the clubhouse by a row of garages. Shading my eyes against the morning sun, I squinted to try and see who had arrived, but the garages and bottle banks blocked my view.

I could feel my stomach bubbling now, and my legs began to feel twitchy. Turning back towards the car to fetch my bag, I realized Dad and Harry were still inside. I opened the door and grinned. "Hey, people, let's go!" I said.

"Harry, for Pete's sake!" Dad was saying.

Harry's face was like thunder. "Told you – I'm not budging! I'm here, aren't I? What more do you want?"

"I can't leave you alone in the car."

Harry waved his hands around. "Dad, I'm thirteen and I'm in the quietest, most boring car park in Britain."

"I don't care. I'm not happy leaving you here all alone. I need to be able to see you."

"Why? You don't need to see me mid-week, do you? It doesn't bother you then, does it? What's the big deal now?"

Dad's voice cracked then. "Harry, that's unfair," he said and he sounded so hurt, but Harry didn't seem to care.

I wondered what I could do to make things OK, but just then Mrs Akboh, Eve's mum, drove up, dumping Eve, Gemma and Amy in a noisy heap next to me. I like Eve's mum. She's a nurse, like Megan's mum, and always seems really happy and cheerful. If I were ever in hospital, I'd want her to look after me. "I'll be back before kick-off!" she called out as she reversed away.

"You'd better be!" Eve replied, waving like crazy.

I closed our car door and waved too, hoping nobody would notice the argument going on behind me.

Eve grinned, holding up her hand for me to slap.

"Yo, Lucy-Lou! It's so long since I saw you! Gimme some skin!"

I rolled my eyes at her. Eve's in my class so it was less than a day since she'd seen me. I high-fived her anyway, then high-fived Gemma and Amy. Neither of them goes to my school so I only knew them from coming here. Out of the two of them I like Gemma better. She's quiet but really skilled – I mean *seriously* skilled. My mum had been at the summer tournament and she had said straight away, "There's your natural." I'm not so keen on Amy. She puts people down and I don't like that. And she's rubbish at football – but only because she doesn't try. It's well annoying having someone like that on the same team as you.

"Hey, Lucy, check these out. How amazing are *they*?" Amy asked me. She pointed to her football boots, which were an immaculate white. "I can't tell you how much they cost," she said – then immediately told me.

"No way!" I replied, not because I was impressed

but because I knew what a rip-off trendy boots like that were.

"Oh yeah." Amy smirked. "Crazy price."

Behind her Eve made "big-head" signs with her hands. I pressed my lips together and tried not to giggle.

"Er ... Lucy," Dad interrupted, winding the window down and leaning towards us, "I'm going to take Harry for a coffee. I'll see you for the kick-off, if you're OK?"

I nodded, relieved they'd stopped arguing.

The four of us joined the others who had already arrived – Hannah and Katie, our ace coaches, and Megan, Petra, Jenny-Jane and Holly from the team. Everyone started talking all at once – they all seemed as hyper as I was. "Why don't you lot go for a jog round the pitch until the rest of them get here?" Hannah suggested.

"Oh, I thought you'd never ask!" Eve joked, and led us away. By the time we'd completed a full circuit, Nika and Tabinda had arrived, and halfway round the second lap the twins, Daisy and Dylan, joined in. The barmy army was complete!

We'd all been fairly quiet at training mid-week; I guess because we were getting used to each other again after the summer break, but now the chatter rose and dipped and rose again as we jogged. I found out all about Holly's holiday in Florida and Nika's stay with her grandparents near Lviv and Eve's birthday party at Alton Towers. Megan was the only one who talked football. "I wish that friendly hadn't been cancelled," she confided. "We could have done with the run-out before facing that lot, especially as we've only had one training session this season."

"I know," I agreed, glancing across to the far side of the pitch where the Grove Belles, last season's cup and league winners, had arrived and were warming up. Just seeing them, uniformly tall and strong in their all-white kit, sent shivers through you. They all looked – well, it sounds silly, but – so professional. I glanced over my shoulder. Holly and Amy had already dropped out, and Dylan and Daisy, the two youngest in the squad, were only walking. It was then I knew we would lose today. If we couldn't even get through the warm-ups, we had no chance. I just hoped it wouldn't be a massacre.

Time flew. Katie did some short drills with us, and before I knew it we were gathered in a huddle, ready for kick-off. I was tingling all over now, despite my gloomy prediction. I linked arms with Nika and Holly as we waited for Hannah to give us our final instructions. "OK, it's a big day for us," she began, "but just remember everything we talked about in training. Mark up in defence. Midfield, I want you helping at the back when needs be. This lot will put pressure on you from the second the ref blows his whistle. And remember, if in doubt…"

"Kick it out," we chorused. Clearing the ball to safety was one of the first things Hannah had taught us.

"Exactly. OK, everyone gets a game. If you're not on first half, you play second half, all right? So, Meggo starts in goal and is captain; Hols and Lucy in defence, with Hols on the left and Lucy on the right." Holly and I smiled at each other. We enjoyed playing together at the back. "… Dayz left midfield, Dyl right midfield…" She paused to point out left to Daisy and right to Dylan, then continued, "Gemma central midfield, and Nika as lone striker."

Nika grinned. I think she liked the idea of being the *lone* striker.

"OK, let's do this, Parsnips!" Hannah whooped.

The circle broke up and there was a cheer from the crowd as we took up our positions. I glanced round and saw my dad and Harry standing among the other parents. Dad grinned and stuck his thumbs in the air, but Harry still looked fed up. Never mind, I thought. I had a game to play.

The Grove Belles won the toss and chose to play towards the bottle-bank end first. We kicked off and Gemma tapped it to Daisy, who passed neatly enough towards Dylan – but the Belles' number 11 intercepted it and nipped the ball away, dribbling unchallenged before passing to their number 7, who was already on the edge of the box. I remembered her from the summer tournament; she was called Becky, I think, and was a pretty smart player – but a bit of a cheat, too. If you went anywhere near her she'd fall over, hoping for a free kick. Holly was meant to be marking her, but she was too slow and the Belles star forward simply swerved round her and had a shot which flew just wide.

Megan took the goal kick and hoofed the ball beyond the halfway line, aiming for Gemma, but it bounced too high and two of the Belles leapt either side of her, barging her out of play and leaving the ball free for the ever-ready Becky to pounce, turn and run with it. From then on we were under siege.

I tried my best to defend the goal, but no matter what I did, nothing seemed to work. I man-marked their number 8, but they simply used other players and scored their first goal with a simple tap-in close to the line.

I then tried protecting Megan by standing near the goal line during the corners, but so did Holly, the twins and Gemma, so we were all bunched up and kept colliding with each other. Megan had to keep shouting at us to get out of her way. "I can't see a thing, people!"

Even with all of us crowding the goalmouth, the Belles found a gap. They scored their second one by slicing the ball through Holly's legs, and the third from a quick corner that looped above all our heads only to be headed in by Becky.

Whenever I did manage to gain possession I did what Hannah had told us to do and immediately kicked the ball out. I heard Dad shout "Well done, Lucy!" a few times, but the trouble was I gave away so many throw-ins and corners by kicking it out that the Belles were always at an advantage and we never got a chance to break forward.

We were losing four–nil at half-time and Becky

had a hat-trick. She walked off, high-fiving her team-mates.

"Keep your heads up, girls," Katie said as we trooped off the pitch. "You're not doing too badly."

I guessed not, but it felt like we were.

I glanced round at everyone. The twins were bickering, Gemma and Nika were leaning dejectedly against each other and Holly was bent double, out of breath and bright red.

"Well, that was fun – not!" Megan stated as everyone grouped together round the coats and bags. "We're giving it to them on a plate again, just like in the tournament." We'd lost seven–one that time.

Hannah clapped her hands and looked stern. "Meggo! No negative talk, please! You're all a bit rusty after the holidays, that's all."

"Yeah, you guys; don't stress," Amy said, bending to flick a blade of grass from her new boots. "It's only a game, remember."

Megan began choking on her water, and I had to

turn away and stare at the hedge behind me. *Only* a game. ONLY! Everyone knew there was no such thing as *only* a game.

I couldn't help feeling disappointed when Amy was put on in my place. I knew Hannah and Katie wanted everyone to have a turn, and that was fair enough, but *Amy*... I just knew she'd be more bothered about not getting her boots dirty than about even *trying* to defend.

I watched the second half from the touchline with Dad and Harry. Harry ignored both of us and spent his time texting. I didn't blame him. We were even worse this half and I was totally right about Amy. She just kept flinching and turning away if the play came anywhere near her. It drove me potty! Jenny-Jane, on for Gemma, was the opposite: she got way too stuck in, hacking away at any Belles ankle she could find, whether the player had the ball or not – so she was always being warned about fouling. That meant as well as throw-ins and corners we were defending from free kicks now. Dad chuckled at her, though. "That's the spirit, flower," he kept saying.

Final score: nine–nil. Not a full-scale massacre, but bad enough.

Hannah called us all together. "OK, gather round. Lucy! Hols! Hursty! Tabs! Over here!"

I left Dad and Harry and ambled across to join the team.

"Right, that's them out of the way. We'll start the season properly next week, OK?"

I suppose that was one way of looking at it.

"Nine! They put *nine* goals past me!" Megan wailed. "I need a hug!"

"I'll hug you!" Eve declared, throwing her arms round her. "Come here, babe! Come to Momma!"

"Me, too! I'll hug you, Megan," Tabinda said, and wrapped her arms round Megan and Eve.

"Hey! She's *my* bezzie!" Petra protested and lunged at them. Soon we were all piling on top of Megan, giggling our heads off.

"Can't breathe! Can't breathe!" Megan squawked from somewhere beneath the bundle.

Hannah and Katie cracked up, too. "What are they like?" Hannah asked Katie.

"Nutters, the lot of them," Katie replied.

"When you clowns have finished, there's one piece of business to do before you go," Hannah told us as we rolled about on the grass. From her sports bag, she pulled out a bronze-coloured trophy. It had a rectangular stumpy base with a tiny football perched on top of it. "I did ask for one with a parsnip on, but they were out of stock!" Hannah joked. "Anyway, I am delighted to say that the first ever Parsnip of the Match award goes to..." She paused and let her eyes roam around the squad until they settled on me. "Lucy Skidmore, for her sterling defending. Well done, mush!"

She held out the trophy for me and I felt my cheeks burn. "Me?" I asked, feeling embarrassed.

"Yes, you!" Hannah nodded. "You, for your awareness on the pitch and for pegging back their number 8 so effectively."

"Thank you," I mumbled as everyone clapped.

☆ MATCH THREE ☆

Teams:
Parrs U11s (Parsnips) v.
Hixton Lees Juniors

Date & venue:
Saturday 15 September
at Lornton FC, Low Road,
Lornton
(home match)

Kick-off:
10.30

Attendance:
19

3

The following Saturday I dressed, did my sock thing, went downstairs, had breakfast, filled my water bottle, packed my stuff and chatted to Mum about her plans for the day – schoolwork and housework; not very thrilling. At least I think that's what she said. If I'm honest, I was only half-listening, because I was even more excited about playing this week than I had been the week before. It's the pits knowing you're going to lose from the start, like I knew we would against the Belles, but Hixton Lees are nowhere near in the same league as the Belles (well, they are in the same actual *league,* but you know what I mean). I'd checked out their points from last season on the website and they'd come bottom! It wasn't that I thought we'd beat them just because of that, but it meant the match would be more even.

The excitement turned to stress when at ten to ten Harry was still in bed and Dad hadn't arrived. I knew why Harry was late – Mum hadn't paid him to get up this time – but I didn't know why Dad was. "You don't think he's been in a crash, do you?" I asked Mum.

Mum shook her head and stirred her coffee. "Of course not! He'll be here any minute."

"And *pleeeeease* will you get Harry up for me? He keeps telling me to get lost when I knock. I'm going to miss all the warm-ups at this rate."

Mum sighed, set her cup down on the worktop and nodded. "I'll try," she said, "though whether I'll get much joy remains to be seen."

Dad arrived just after Mum had gone upstairs. "Roadworks," he snapped before I'd even had a chance to ask. He then immediately returned to the car to wait. It was another five minutes before Harry appeared, hair all over the place, scowling and silent.

He slid into the front seat and pulled his seatbelt on without saying a thing. Dad didn't say anything either, so it was up to me to fill the gaps. It was either that or sit in silence and I couldn't bear that.

By the time we arrived at the ground I was all talked out. I was also late – well, my version of late, not Daisy and Dylan McNeil's version of late. I only had ten minutes till kick-off, so this time I didn't wait for Dad when he parked up. I just checked there were no cars behind me, jumped out, yelled "See you in a bit!" and pelted across to the field.

The team were just finishing shooting practice. "Sorry, sorry, sorry," I panted, feeling deflated when they stopped and began gathering all the balls up the second I arrived.

"Don't worry, Lucy; you're here now." Hannah smiled.

"Put this on," Katie said, and handed me a yellow tabard. "Hixton are in red, too."

I nodded, pulling the tabard over my head, hoping I'd be chosen to start the match – but I wasn't.

My heart sank as Hannah fired off the list: Megan in goal, Petra and Jenny-Jane at the back, with Nika in the central midfield position assisted by Gemma on the left and Daisy on the right. Amy was up front for some reason; Hannah usually played her at the back with us. "OK, we're going to be rotating you this week, so you'll all be on for only about fifteen minutes at a time until your fitness levels are up."

I watched with envy as my team took up their positions. I pulled my fleece on over my kit and gave my dad a quick smile as he and Harry came to stand near by. Dad, who seemed a bit more relaxed now, winked at me, but Harry just looked miserable.

Hixton kicked off. Their midfielder was a small girl with dark hair and glasses. She tapped the ball to her partner on the right, who unintentionally kicked it straight at Nika. The ball bounced off Nika's knees, and then there was a tussle between her and their number 9. Number 9 won the ball, ran with it for a couple of metres, saw Jenny-Jane bearing down on her and kicked the ball into touch, even though she had someone free in the middle. Jenny-Jane has that effect on people! Jenny-Jane went to take the throw-in, twisting one way, then the other, waiting for someone to break free. "Help her out, one of you!" Katie yelled.

Gemma ran forward and called for the ball. Jenny-Jane lobbed it at her and she cushioned it on her thigh, bringing it down and under control so smoothly, so swiftly, in a way she hadn't been allowed to by the Belles last week. Oh, she was so good!

"Go Gemma Hurst!" Eve shouted as Gemma swerved round one of the Hixton defenders and squared it to Daisy. I closed one eye then, because you never knew what Daisy would do, but actually she simply passed back to Gemma, who was by now on the edge of the penalty area. Gemma struck the ball hard, but it sailed just too high and bounced off the crossbar and over the netting for a goal kick. All the parents on our side clapped and ooohed and Hannah yelled out, "Fantastic attempt, Hursty!"

For the next few minutes it was all a bit scrappy, with both sides gaining possession and then instantly losing it again. We seemed to have more chances, but somehow we never scored.

After ten minutes it was still nil-all, and then the Hixton goalie booted the ball out to the right wing. It didn't land near anyone, so there was a race to see who could get to it first. Nika won, but she slipped and fell, so a grateful Hixton midfielder dribbled the ball down the line. She stopped well outside the box, but had a shot anyway. The ball sailed high in the air, and it wouldn't have gone in if Petra hadn't leapt for it and headed it the wrong way for an own goal. Poor Petra! She clapped her hands over her mouth and began apologizing to Megan, who just patted her as if to say "No worries." I felt so sorry for Petra. I knew exactly how she felt – I'd done the same when we played the Lornton Under 10s boys' team back in April.

"Never mind! Never mind! Play on!" Hannah urged.

The goal seemed to put a spell on both sides. A good spell on Hixton – they began passing the ball better – and a bad spell on us: we became pants. Within five minutes Hixton's number 9 had scored twice, despite Megan making some brilliant stops in between. The spectators on the Hixton side were jumping up and down in celebration as if they'd won the lottery or something.

Hannah then made four substitutions. I was on for Petra. "Mark number 9," Katie whispered to me.

I nodded, tingling all over as I waited for Petra to come off. Yes! Finally!

"Up and at 'em, petal," Dad called out as I ran on to take up my position.

"Thanks, Dad." I grinned.

Harry just glowered.

Number 9 took me by surprise by beaming at me when I stood next to her. The Grove Belles girl hadn't spoken to me at all. "Hello," she said, "I'm Aisha."

"Lucy."

"I've scored two goals!"

"I know."

"Isn't it great?"

I stared at her. What was I meant to say to that? Congratulations?

"Soz, that sounds really big-headed! It's just I've never scored before, and we always lost last season so it's just so cool to be winning."

"I guess it must be."

"We beat the other new team six–nil last week – and now you."

I frowned. "You mean Southfields?"

"Uh-huh. Southfields Athletic, except they weren't athletic they were more … *path*letic."

I felt annoyed then. It must feel great winning matches for the first time, but it wasn't very sporting to brag about beating inexperienced teams. Everyone has to start somewhere.

☆ ☆ ☆

I went in quick and keen. I stuck to Aisha and made sure whenever the ball came near her I was there first, darting just in front of her every time and clearing the ball out of danger. "Well played, Lucy!" I could hear my dad yelling every two seconds.

"The other girl didn't do that," Aisha complained after I'd intercepted another pass. She didn't seem quite so gleeful now.

I was just beginning to relax into the game when the whistle went for half-time. Half-time already! I'd only just got going!

"How was that?" Hannah asked as we gathered in a semicircle by our bottles and bags.

"I don't get it. We're playing better than last week but we're still losing," Tabinda moaned.

Hannah laughed. "That's football for you! The main thing is you *are* playing better – a thousand times better – so just keep doing what you're doing and you'll be fine."

"What's great is that you're all trying so hard," Katie added.

Hannah made a few changes but I was allowed to stay on, which boosted me no end. I took up my position next to Aisha.

"Hello again, Lucy," she said. You had to hand it to her, she was pally!

"Hello again, Aisha."

"This is a good game, isn't it?"

"It's about to get even better," I told her.

Guess what? I was right! It got much better because we scored twice in the first seven minutes! Once from a corner and once in a goalmouth scramble. Nika scored both. Go Nika! The goals totally deflated Hixton, and for the next ten minutes the ball was ours. I lost count of the number of shots we had on target until we scored again – and when we did it was a beauty from Gemma. She simply flicked the ball between the keeper's legs – a perfect nutmeg. Three-all!

"Bum," Aisha said to me.

"Sorry," I said, trying not to grin too much.

But then we – or, if I'm honest, *I* – blew it. They had a goal kick after another of our near misses. The goalie wellied the ball any old how, but it landed flukily right at the feet of their dark-haired midfielder. She dribbled the ball forward and crossed it low into the box. I had Aisha pegged back, and Holly was blocking another of their players – but their number 21 was totally unmarked. As she got herself into striking position I saw Jenny-Jane hare towards her with such a fierce look on her face it worried me.

"Don't foul her, JJ!" I shouted, scared we'd give away a penalty if she did – and Jenny-Jane reared back long enough for the Hixton player not only to shoot but also to score.

"Yes!" Aisha yelled and did an impressive cartwheel.

Hannah made the final substitutions soon afterwards. Both Jenny-Jane and I were brought off.

"Sorry," I said to Jenny-Jane. "I just thought…"

"Yeah, well, you thought wrong, Miss Perfect!" she muttered.

The final score was four–three to them.

Hannah tried to cheer us all up during the warm-down. She went round each one of us telling us how well we'd done. "Lucy – excellent defending again this week," she said to me, but I just wanted the ground to swallow me whole. Nika won the Parsnip of the Match trophy. At least she deserved it.

☆ MATCH FOUR ☆

Teams:
Parrs U11s (Parsnips) v.
Southfields Athletic

Date & venue:
Thursday 20 September
at Dale Field, Southfields

Kick-off:
18.00

Attendance:
11

4

This match was on a Thursday evening.

That meant Dad wouldn't be around to take me, and Mum couldn't either because she had a Year Nine parents' evening. To make things even more complicated, I also had a netball match straight after school.

I don't do complicated; it unsettles me. Luckily Eve plays netball, too, so she said her mum would pick us up after the match and we could have tea in town on the way to Southfields. Mum arranged to fetch me from Eve's house afterwards.

Then there was all the Harry stuff. To be fair, it was complicated for Harry, too, because he was in Year Nine, and Mum would be tied up talking to all the parents about their kids' progress in PE, so she wouldn't be able to go round asking about her own son's progress in everything else. That meant either Dad had to come from Bicester after work to do it, or she would just have to ask about Harry in the staffroom later. Harry told Dad not to bother coming because he didn't care what the stupid teachers thought of him anyway, but Dad said in that case he'd definitely be attending.

To make it clear for everyone, Mum wrote all the arrangements down on the whiteboard in her study, and that helped. There were two columns: one for me, one for Harry.

I copied my instructions down on a piece of paper and folded it into my jotter, just to be sure, including the bit about reminding Dad to pick us up on Friday. Deep down I knew Dad would never forget something as important as taking us to Bicester for the first time. I knew he was really looking forward to showing us his new flat. Writing everything down took ages. You'll see why when you look at the list.

Thursday 20 September
After-school arrangements

Lucy	Harry
3.30 netball (take kit – good luck)	3.30 Homework Club (take pack-up for tea)
4.20 go with Eve (take money for dinner and offer to pay)	5.30 Dad arrives – meet in main entrance. He'll text u if he's late. Your first appointment is with Miss Gilbert at 5.40
5.15 ish travel to Southfields (take kit)	
6.00 football (win this time!)	6.45 your last appointment – maths with Mr Strazinzki – don't miss
7.30 ish to Eve's house, Mum will pick up around 7.45 (do homework at Eve's if u have any)	
*Remind Dad he's picking you up Friday for weekend *	*Remind Dad he's picking you up Friday for weekend *

☆ ☆ ☆

The netball-match bit was easy-peasy. We drew six-all, and Eve was happy because she's goal shooter and scored four, and I was happy because, well, as you know, I *loooove* playing sport!

The journey into town was cool, too. Mrs Akboh made us laugh by telling us about a man who'd come into A and E with a pan stuck on his head and peas all down his neck.

"No way!" I said. "How come?"

"I've learned never to ask," she replied.

"Oh."

"But speaking of dozy things, we're meeting Samuel and Claude in McDonald's. I hope that's OK with you, Lucy? They wanted to watch Eve play."

Samuel and Claude are Eve's brothers. "Sure. I'd like to meet them."

"They'd like to meet you, too. Your dad was one of their favourite teachers."

"I get that a lot." I beamed.

"I bet you're missing him."

I nodded and felt a lump come to my throat.

"How's your mum?" she asked swiftly.

"OK, thanks. A bit tired."

"I hope you're helping with the chores?"

"Every night," I replied. "I set the table for dinner and unload the dishwasher."

"Sounds like me!" Eve interrupted. "Only I get to iron my own clothes too. Isn't it divine?"

Mrs Akboh pulled up outside McDonald's and pinched Eve's cheek. "And I appreciate it, Evie-girl. Being a single parent is full-on twenty-four-seven. We mums need all the help from our chicks we can get."

I remembered then that Eve's dad had died when she was little. At school she always talks about him as if he were still alive, so I'd never thought of Mrs Akboh as being a single parent, too, like my mum and my dad. There's more of them out there than you realize!

"Chicks? Do I look like a chick to you?" Eve complained. "Am I covered in yellow down? Am I so cute you want to bite my head off? I don't think so."

"Evie, stop talking and get walking," Mrs Akboh
told her.

Claude and Samuel had saved us a corner table
by the stairs. I knew straight away they were Eve's
brothers: they both had the same wide, brown eyes
and funky hairstyle as Eve – long straight cornrows
tied in a neat knot at the back. I wished my hair was
curly like theirs and could be done like that.

It was fun just eating and chatting, but halfway
through our tea a gang of teenagers came clattering
down the stairs, screeching and pushing each
other and swearing like mad. Samuel stopped
mid-sentence because he couldn't be heard, and
my heart stopped mid-beat when I realized that
the gang member doing the most screeching and
pushing and swearing was my brother, Harry.

I was so surprised to see him I shot up out of
my seat, making Eve jump. "Harry?" I called after
him. He didn't hear, so I rushed after him before

he could leave. *"Harry!"*

One of the girls he was with nudged him in the back. "Haz, someone wants you."

He turned, his face lit up and happy in a way I hadn't seen for ages. Then he saw me – and it was as if there'd been a power cut. "What do you want?" he snapped.

"I … you should be at Homework Club."

The gang round him burst into laughter. "Harry, you naughty boy! You should be at Homework Club! Why aren't you at Homework Club? Hang your head in shame!"

"Shurrup!" Harry told them.

"You'll miss Dad, won't you?" I asked, trying to ignore the others. I didn't recognize any of them apart from the two girls. They were the ones who'd blown kisses at Harry the last time we were in here.

What I said made them all laugh even more. "Aw! Harry's missing his daddy! Poor ickle Harry." One of the boys pulled at Harry's cheek and wobbled it.

Harry brushed his hand away angrily. "Back off, Arron!' he told the boy. By now Harry's face was deep red and I was feeling more and more uncomfortable. He narrowed his eyes at me. "FYI Dad's not coming. Something's" – Harry paused to bend his index fingers into quotation marks – "'cropped up', so butt out, OK? And keep out of my face – or else!"

I blinked and tried not to well up. Harry was never usually this mean to me.

Mrs Akboh patted the back of my hand as I sat down, and Claude let out the loudest burp ever. His eyes flew open before his mum could tell him off. "Sorry! I didn't mean it, Ma! It came out louder than I planned!" he protested, hooting with laughter and high-fiving Samuel.

"Are all brothers foul?" Eve asked me.

I twisted in my chair to see if Harry was still around, but he'd disappeared. "I guess," I said, drawing circles in the spilt salt on the tabletop.

☆ ☆ ☆

The incident with Harry upset me quite a bit. I kept replaying it over and over in my head, seeing his angry face and narrowed eyes, so many times that it wasn't until Eve nudged my arm that I realized the car had stopped and we'd arrived.

"Calling Lucy Skidmore! Calling Lucy Skidmore! Come in, please!" Eve laughed, wiggling her fingers in front of my face.

"Sorry!"

We piled out of the car and looked around. Dale Field, Southfield Athletic's ground, was just that. One field with one pitch bang in the middle. To our left was a drab grey changing block with rusty bars over the window. It made Lornton FC look swanky.

"I remember now" – Claude sniffed – "we've played here. Watch out for dog mess on the pitch."

"Nice," Eve replied, hiking her kit bag over her shoulder.

"Come on," Mrs Akboh said, "you girls had better get changed."

"We'll carry out a pitch inspection," Samuel said and walked off with Claude.

I shook myself to get focused for the match. Forget Harry, I told myself. Think football.

The away team had to change in the kitchen, which was full of stacked plastic chairs and smelled mouldy. "I like what they've done to the place," Eve joked as we joined the others.

"It's so scutty!" said Amy, sniffing the air. "We'll probably catch MRSA or something."

"Keep your voice down, Amy," Hannah warned her. "It's not the club's fault. There's not a lot of money around here."

"Obviously," Amy muttered.

Hannah zipped up her tracksuit top and rubbed her hands together. "OK, everyone. Thanks for coming mid-week; I know it's difficult straight from school. Everyone get here without any hassle?"

I bent to fasten my boots properly and sighed. If only!

"Katie's got to work tonight, so it's just me, but

she sends her love and says she expects a text at seven o'clock telling her you played brilliantly. Deal or no deal?"

"Deal!" we chorused.

"That's the ticket, girls! Just a word about the pitch before we go out there. As you'll notice, the far side slopes down onto a road. There's no fencing, and I don't want to see any of you running after the ball down there? OK? Daisy? Dylan?"

"Yessir," they replied.

"Leave it for one of the adults to fetch. Right, then. Let's go and get those three points."

Hannah chose me as one of the starters, thank goodness. I was glad to be given a chance to get going right away so that I could run off Harry's nastiness. "Defence OK again, Lucy? You played a blinder last week. Mark their number 10."

I nodded. Fine by me.

Number 10 had short, light brown hair and was wearing the captain's armband.

"Hi," I said, thinking I'd be friendly to her like Aisha had been to me.

She looked at me glumly. "Hi," she said.

I did a quad stretch to keep warmed up. "Are you ... er ... looking forward to it?"

"To what?"

"Playing."

"Not really. We'll only get thrashed again."

"You might not," I said. "We haven't won yet either."

She bucked up then. "Haven't you?"

"No."

"Right," she said and rolled up her sleeves. "Oi, you lot, we're in with a chance – this lot ain't won yet neither!" she called out in a booming voice that carried all the way across Dale Field.

Cringe! I didn't dare look around to see what the reaction to *that* was!

"Whenever you're ready, Crystal," the ref called.

"Any time," a chirpy Crystal replied.

☆ ☆ ☆

I needn't have worried. This might sound mean, but we'd have had to have our legs tied together to lose to Southfields. They were just not very good at holding onto the ball, or doing anything with it when they did have it. Most of their kicking was so wild the ball ended up on the road more than on the pitch, and in the end one of the parents stayed down there, hidden in the dip, for the whole match.

Eve, as lone striker, scored two in the first three minutes, and Gemma and Nika one each a few minutes after that. "Thought you said you was rubbish," Crystal muttered to me as the ball was set up on the centre spot again.

"No, I said we hadn't won yet."

"Huh!"

It ended seven–nil to us. "Oh well, we didn't do too bad in the end," Crystal said with a shrug during the three cheers. "We lost twelve–nil to them Vixens last week."

"We lost nine–nil to the Belles."

"Oh Gawd!" Crystal said, drawing her finger

across her throat and going cross-eyed. "I'm
throwing a sickie when we plays them!"

Back in the changing room, Eve was awarded
Parsnip of the Match. She was so funny about it!
"Me? Seriously? Me? Little old Eve Akboh? Oh,
I can't possibly accept!" she said, snatching the
statue from Hannah's hand. "But now that I have,
I'd like to say a few thank-yous. First of all, thank
you to my feet for scoring the goals today. I couldn't
have done it without you. Thank you to the grass
for..." She stopped and sniffed. "What's that smell?"

"Is this part of the speech?" Daisy asked.

"Thank you to the grass for growing," Dylan said
helpfully.

Eve shook her head, her nose wrinkling. "No.
Something smells *gross*..."

We all began sniffing. She was right. "Uh-oh.
Boot check, everyone," Hannah instructed.

Guess who'd trodden in dog poo and trailed
it into the changing room? Amy Minter. She was

furious! "My new boots!" she kept shrieking, staring at the brown-caked soles in disgust. "They cost a fortune! I'm so going to sue!"

Hannah wrapped the boots in a sheet of old newspaper and then put them in a carrier bag. "You'll still have to take them home with you, sweetheart."

Poor Amy. It wasn't a very nice thing to happen – but it was funny. Every time Eve and I started talking about it on the way home, we cracked up laughing. "I'm going to sue!" Eve kept repeating, as she polished her trophy with her sleeve. "I'm so going to sue!"

Mum picked me up from Eve's at about half-past seven. Harry was in the back of the car. "Hi, everybody," I said, still giddy from laughing so much. Harry twisted away as soon as he saw me and stared out of the window. I gave Mum a hug because she looked exhausted. "Hello, best mum in the world," I said. "How did parents' evening go?"

"Oh, it went fine," Mum said, her voice as sharp as a papercut, "considering your brother has had me out of my mind with worry all evening."

I drew back. "What do you mean?"

"I mean he decided not to go to Homework Club and didn't bother to tell anyone, so when your father arrived he didn't know where Harry was and nor did I."

"But Dad couldn't come," I mumbled.

"Oh, that's what Harry told you, is it?" Mum growled.

"And I told you that's what Dad told me!" Harry growled back.

I swallowed hard as my stomach cramped. Why did the beginning and end of every match have to be like this? Why couldn't everything be fun, like with Eve's family?

☆ MATCH FIVE ☆

Teams:
Parrs U11s (Parsnips) v.
Cuddlethorpe Tigers

Date & venue:
Sunday 23 September
at Lornton FC, Low Road,
Lornton
(home match)

Kick-off:
11.00

Attendance:
19

This match felt different. For a start, it was on a Sunday and I was coming all the way from Bicester for it. We'd had to get up so early to get to Lornton (half-six to be out by half-seven), and that hadn't helped on the grumpy front with Harry. Not that he could have got much grumpier. Things were still tense from the parents' evening on Thursday, and they'd become even more tense when we arrived in King's End the next evening and Harry had seen Dad's new flat.

"Is this it?" he asked in disbelief as soon as we'd stepped inside and dumped our bags on Dad's bed, which was in the only room.

"There's a separate kitchen and bathroom," Dad pointed out.

I have to say, like Harry, I felt a little disappointed.

From the outside it had looked as if Dad had a huge old house on three storeys, and I had got all excited thinking I'd have loads of rooms to explore, but it turned out he only had part of the building, on the ground floor, and I wasn't allowed up the stairs because other people lived in that bit.

"So this is the lot?" Harry asked again, frowning. "No garden? No spare bedroom?"

"This is the lot!" Dad said, a brave smile on his face. "Small, but cosy."

"I like it," I fibbed.

"It's adequate," Dad said. "And it's cheap. It means we don't have to sell the house, so you can all stay in Meadow Crescent." He looked at Harry when he said that.

"What, so all three of us have to sleep in here? You've got to be kidding!" Harry fumed.

"Don't worry – the sofa turns into a bed, and I've got an inflatable mattress for one of you. No one has to share."

"It sucks!"

"I'll sleep on the mattress," I said quickly, hoping Harry would stop grumbling then.

"'I'll sleep on the mattress,'" Harry mimicked. "Tch! You're such a creep, Lucy."

That kind of set the tone for the rest of the weekend.

The journey to Lornton on Sunday morning seemed to take for ever, especially with everyone being fed up. It wasn't until Dad turned into Low Road and I saw the clubhouse that I brightened. Holly waved to me as we crossed the grass, and it felt good to know I had people I could talk to who would answer me nicely instead of making me feel bad for even opening my mouth. "I'll go and get ready, if that's OK," I said to Dad.

"You do that, sweetheart," Dad said.

I didn't even look at Harry. There was no point.

Throwing my bag and water bottle down on top of everyone else's, I joined in with the pre-match chat. Tabinda was telling everyone about her spoilt cousins who'd spent the weekend with them. "They wanted to play on the Wii all the time, right, but when I beat them they got the hump, so Mum said I had to let them win. Charming! I wouldn't mind, but they're way older than me…"

I smiled, glad I wasn't the only one with irritating relatives.

The Cuddlethorpe Tigers arrived just as we were doing our stretches. They were the team who'd dropped out of the pre-season friendly with us. I liked their blue and white striped shirts. Red versus blue. My two favourite colours. Man U v. Everton or Chelsea. Yes! I began jumping up and down on the spot and felt the adrenalin rush kick in. This was more like it. Blow that whistle, ref, please!

Speaking of refs, Katie had that job today, so she couldn't join us for our pep talk. It was down to Hannah to big us up on her own. "OK," she began, "we're missing Amy today because she hasn't found any new boots yet…"

"She could have just cleaned her others!" Jenny-Jane grunted. "All you have to do is wait till the poo goes hard and then scrape it off with a knife."

"For good advice and all household tips, see Miss Bayliss!" Hannah laughed.

"I was just sayin'." Jenny-Jane scowled, not liking being teased.

Hannah glanced at her clipboard. "OK, the twins are late…"

"Never!" Megan scoffed.

"Amazing!" Holly added.

"All right, ladies… Thank you…" Hannah warned. I've noticed Hannah is tolerant of lateness but not so tolerant of us dissing our team-mates. That makes a good coach, I think. "… and Nika and Eve are at church…" she continued, before pausing for a second to look at us all. "Is there anyone else who finds Sunday matches difficult to get to? I'll try to bring it up when we arrange the fixtures next time if it is a problem."

I wondered whether to say anything about the

early start I'd had to make, but I didn't think Hannah would count that as a problem, so I kept quiet.

"OK," she continued. "You all played brilliantly on Thursday. Your passing was much better; you were thinking about finding space and you were more aware of one another. All signs of a team that's coming together."

"Southfields *let* us find space, though," Tabinda pointed out.

"Well, let's see if the Tigers do!" Hannah smiled. "Go get 'em!"

Considering how fed up I'd been earlier, this match turned out to be my best game yet! It was utterly butterly! Hannah put me at the back with Holly and Petra again for the whole of the first half. "Stay with their number 11," were my orders. Number 11 looked titchy; she would probably only come up to my armpit. Oh well. Being tall wasn't something I could control.

Katie blew her whistle and we kicked off. I don't know what it was, but there was a different feeling in the air today. Everyone seemed so – I don't know – up for it, I suppose. We chased every ball, and if we lost it we chased it again until we regained it. Holly was much better at intercepting passes this week. I reckon she'd finally worked off all the hot dogs she'd had in Disneyland!

After five minutes we were one–nil up and after ten, two–nil, with Nika netting the first and Tabinda the second. When Cuddlethorpe had possession, they tried to pass to my number 11 every time. Sometimes she got the ball and sometimes I did, but the times she did have possession I marked her so tightly she ended up backed into the corner with nowhere to go. "Wake up, Serena! What's the matter with you?" a man on the touchline kept barking at her.

Once in frustration she kicked the ball straight at me. It rebounded off my shin and went out of play for a throw-in. The same man, stout with a black beanie hat pulled over his ears, grabbed the ball and shoved it hard into Serena's arms. "Now, think!

Think!" he said, jabbing his finger angrily into the side of his head.

Serena looked upset as she leapt, trying to throw the ball over my head. I leapt at the same time – but before I could get my head to it, Katie blew the whistle. "Foul throw-in. Take it again, please, Cuddlethorpe."

"What? What?" the man shouted.

Katie kicked the ball gently towards Serena. "Both feet on the ground, please."

"Oh! Another biased ref! That's all we need," he muttered.

Katie ignored him and waited patiently for Serena to get ready. She managed to keep both feet on the ground this time, but the throw landed right in front Jenny-Jane. Jenny-Jane ran with the ball, wriggled clear of two players in midfield and should have passed to Gemma, who was unmarked on the left, but instead she kept running and lost the ball to a good tackle by their defender, right on the edge of the box.

"Never mind, JJ," Hannah said. "Keep trying."

For the rest of that half and most of the second, we dominated. I still stuck with Serena, even though we didn't have much to do. Despite that, the man kept giving her instructions. "Start running *to* it, Serena! You're just spectatin'! Get down there and help your midfield out! What's the matter with you?"

She just stared straight ahead, pretending not to notice.

"Is that your coach?" I whispered.

"No, it's my dad," she muttered, "and I wish he'd drop dead."

I felt so sorry for her having a dad like that. I knew that even if I played like a plank and let in ten own goals, mine would always support me.

It was four–one to us in the end. That meant two wins in a row! "You girls do know you're becoming quite impressive, don't you?" Hannah told us.

"Course we do! We rock!" said Megan matter-of-factly.

"Indeed! Anyway, there's just one tiny thing to do before you all go and tuck into your Yorkshires…" Hannah said, producing another trophy from her bag.

We waited. Receiving the Parsnip of the Match award was becoming a highlight of each game now. I knew I wouldn't get it again so soon and I didn't expect it. Tabinda nudged Petra, who nudged Megan – but it was Jenny-Jane Hannah turned to.

"To our little terrier." Hannah smiled.

Jenny-Jane looked at the trophy suspiciously. "What am I meant to do with this?"

"Put it on your mantelpiece."

"Me mam'll only chuck it at me if I do!" Jenny-Jane muttered.

OK, getting the trophy was a highlight for *some* of us!

☆ MATCH SIX ☆

Teams:
Parrs U11s (Parsnips) v.
Tembridge Vixens

Date & venue:
Saturday 6 October
at Tembridge FC, Station Road,
Tembridge

Kick-off:
10.30

Attendance:
23 (−2 by half-time)

The Friday before the next match started off OK. In fact, it was almost like old times, but with three of us instead of four sitting round the table chatting. Mum had made Harry and me laugh by telling us about a Year Eight girl who'd drawn spots on her feet in red felt pen to try and get out of doing cross-country.

"But why?" I asked in amazement.

"Because not everybody loves PE like you do!" Mum smiled.

"Loads of girls in my form hate it," Harry said. "They're worried their hair will get spoilt or their make-up'll run."

"Hair? What's their hair got to do with cross-country?" I asked.

"Exercise makes it all greasy, doesn't it?"

"Who cares about stuff like that?"

"You will. Trust me."

"I won't."

"Will."

"Won't!"

"Don't tease, Harry," Mum told him.

Harry shrugged. "Why not? What's the point of having a little sister if I can't tease it?"

"'It'? Thanks a lot!" I laughed.

Then Harry asked Mum a question. "You know next weekend?" he said.

"Yes."

"Are you around?"

"As far as I know. Why?"

"Well, Arron's having this party at his house…"

Uh-oh. Alarm bells ringing! Harry was still grounded after parents' evening. This conversation was not going to have a happy ending.

"And?" Mum asked, her mouth tightening.

"Well, I was wondering if I could come back here after, to sleep."

Mum's mouth tightened even more. "No, Harry. Absolutely and definitely not."

No prizes for guessing how Harry reacted. The relaxed atmosphere completely vanished. "Fine, I'll stay over at Arron's instead," he snarled, pushing his plate away.

"You will not!" Mum snarled back. "You are grounded!"

"'Snot up to you, though, is it? Weekends are Dad's look-out. And he'll say yes. He's not an uptight freak like you."

I heard Mum's quick intake of breath and I knew that Harry had gone too far this time.

"Go to your room, Harry," she said in a quiet voice that was still somehow quite scary.

"Make me!" Harry replied, shooting out of his chair and sending it flying backwards into the glass door. I gasped and then held my breath for a second, in case the glass shattered, but the chair just bounced off it and landed upright. "Go on!" Harry goaded. "Make me!"

My legs started to tremble and I felt really, really sick. I hated scenes like this. It had been the same for months and months. "Please don't argue, Harry," I begged, *"please."*

He looked at me with such distaste I felt myself shrivel; then he turned and stormed out.

"Why is he so mean?" I asked Mum.

"It's just a phase," Mum soothed, "just a phase."

I expected Harry to be vile the next morning, too, but actually he was OK. He even asked me who we were playing and what we reckoned our chances were.

"Um … the Tembridge Vixens," I said, "and they're pretty decent – but we've won two in a row, so it could go either way."

I waited, half-expecting him to come out with something cutting, but he just bit into his toast and mumbled, "Well, good luck."

He was even more cheerful with Dad. "Morning, Pops," he greeted, sliding into the front seat and tuning the radio to Radio One.

"Hang on! What's wrong with Radio Two?"
Dad asked.

"It's for old people," Harry replied.

"Oh" – Dad laughed – "and Radio One is for..."

"Cool people, obviously."

"Obviously."

Finally I relaxed. Everything was going to be OK. I could concentrate on thinking about the game against the Tembridge Vixens instead of wondering if Harry was going to throw a hissy fit again. My foot started tapping nervously on the car floor. Kick-off couldn't come fast enough.

As soon as we arrived, I peered across the pitch to where the Vixens were gathered. I did this automatically now. I liked to suss out the enemy. The Vixens played in black and white stripes, like Newcastle and Notts County; it gave them a crisp, sharp look, like a freshly painted fence. Their coach was laughing at something one of the Vixens had told him. I remembered him from the summer tournament; he'd been really friendly and had shouted out compliments to us as well as to his own players. I felt my stomach bubble with excitement. This was going to be a good match. I could feel it in my bones.

We had a full squad today; even Daisy and Dylan managed to make the end of the warm-up drills. Hannah began firing off instructions. "Hols, Lucy and Wardy, I want you at the back. Lucy, watch that number 9... They call her Ninja and she's fast... Megan, I want to hear you shouting orders to your defence... Keep them alert."

"OK Boss! I'm on it!" Megan yelled at the top of her voice and everybody fell about laughing.

As we walked onto the pitch for kick-off I glanced across at Dad and Harry, hoping for a thumbs-up, but they had their backs to the touchline and I could tell from the angle of their heads and Dad's gesticulations that they were arguing. What had happened now? After they'd had such a laugh on the journey over...

I sighed and focused on the game ahead. Hannah

had told me to mark Ninja, the number 9. That's what I'd do.

The Vixens kicked off and the match was under way. Their experience showed instantly. They were much better than us at quick passing, so the ball moved into our half and towards the goalmouth in an instant. I did my best to jockey Ninja, a slim girl with shoulder-length red hair. Hannah was right – she was fast. She knew where I was all the time and she was constantly zigzagging round me. "Mark up! Mark up!" Megan yelled.

Funnily enough, we scored first. They had an attempt on goal but it hit the post, bounced off Holly's chest and landed straight at Jenny-Jane's feet. She hoofed it away – I think aiming just to clear it – but it landed near the centre spot, where an unmarked Nika dribbled it forward. Two Vixens tried to close her down, but Gemma was running parallel and Nika passed it across. Gemma's marker tried to tackle but Gemma leapt over her foot, taking the ball with her, hared forward, then crossed the ball perfectly for Eve in the box. I couldn't see exactly what happened then because the Vixens defence had regrouped and there were black and white stripes everywhere. A second later, though, it was our red shirts who were punching the air in delight and Eve was doing a jig. "Quality! Quality!" I heard the Vixens coach comment, clapping his hands.

The goal seemed to press an alarm button for the Vixens. Their passing became more controlled and their coach began calling out instructions as he followed play up and down the touchline. It wasn't long before he seemed to be near me all the time. "One of you in the middle! One of you! Support Ninja!"

Competing with the Vixens coach was Megan, who had taken Hannah's instructions seriously and was bellowing for Britain. "Hols, move out of my way! Dayz, go forward! Forward! No, not that far! Stay on the flipping pitch! Wardy – near post. Near post!"

I could feel my heart beating in my chest and my stomach doing somersaults. This was so tense! I had to concentrate on Ninja every second. I must have been doing a fairly good job, because she hadn't had that much of the ball – but then suddenly she started waving like mad. "To me, Gazza! To me!" she yelled.

I frowned. We were pretty close to the corner flag and there was no room for a pass. Confused, I turned and prepared to intercept, but the ball was played into a space well to my right and nowhere near us. Ninja suddenly spun the other way, sprinting diagonally, straight to the waiting ball. I chased after her, but too late – she had already passed back to Gazza, an equally pacy forward.

Gazza now darted round Petra and was in the box. I ran in, but Megan had already committed herself by lunging straight at Gazza who, equally committed, couldn't stop her boot clattering against Megan's shin like a hammer meeting wood. I winced as Megan fell to the ground and rolled over in agony, clutching her leg.

Hannah ran on with the first-aid bag as we all crowded round, including their coach and Gazza, who was saying, "Are you all right? I'm so sorry!"

"I'm fine, honest; I'm fine!" Megan protested, but she was biting her lower lip, trying not to cry.

"Come off, Meggo," Hannah ordered. Megan shook her head stubbornly, but Hannah wouldn't listen. She hoisted Megan up and began leading her off the pitch. "Hols, take over in goal," she instructed over her shoulder.

"Me?" Holly asked. "But I can't kick very far."

"Lucy will take the goal kicks; you defend the net."

"OK," said Holly and looked at me in dread.

"You'll be great," I told her.

The ref blew her whistle. Thinking she meant start, I placed the ball on the edge of the box and prepared to take my first ever goal kick – but the ref blew again.

"Wait for your new player," she instructed as Amy strode onto the pitch in her flash new boots – bright orange ones this time – and took up her position next to Ninja.

"You've got to mark the one Holly was marking," Amy told me as she passed.

"Got you," I said, and prepared to take the free kick again – only for the ref to whistle *again*. Not once but several times, shrill and impatient. I scowled and glanced towards the touchline. What now?

What I saw killed every somersault in my stomach stone dead. Harry was stomping across the field, with the ref trotting after him, blowing her whistle and telling him to get off the pitch. "What're you doing?" she called. "There's a match going on here if you hadn't noticed, matey!" Harry wasn't listening. His face was contorted with rage as he strode towards me. I stood rooted to the spot, my palms prickling, wondering what he was going to do. Scream at me? Call me names? Punch me, even?

Anything was possible these days.

In the end, he simply blanked me. Walked straight past as if I were invisible, and totally blanked me. As he passed, though, he blasted the ball from near my feet. I held my breath... The ball seemed certain to hit somebody. Luckily, it flew between the spectators and bounced behind them. "Watch it!" the Vixens coach told him, but Harry just ploughed on without speaking, without stopping, like a car whose brakes had failed.

The spectators parted to allow him through. From the corner of my eye I saw Dad on the other side, half striding, half running round the outer edge of the pitch. He was waving to me and holding up my bag, gesticulating that I should follow him. Confused, I glanced across to Hannah, but she was busy examining Megan's shin. It was Katie who nodded at me to go. Already Daisy was running on to take my place.

I could feel everyone staring at me, wondering what was going on. "I've got to take over," Daisy said apologetically when I didn't move, "'cos your brother's gone twaddly."

"I know," I whispered. I dropped my head to hide the stinging in my eyes and quickly darted through the gap the crowd had made, running to catch up with Dad and Harry.

Harry had stormed straight past our car and was headed out towards the main road. We shouted after him, but instead of waiting he broke into a run. I tried chasing after him, but my studs held me back and by the time I'd bent to undo the laces, Harry was already out of sight and Dad was papping his horn, yelling at me to get into the car.

"What's going on?" I asked as I clipped in my seatbelt with shaky hands. "Why is he running away?"

"Why? Why?" Dad asked, his face set hard. "Because, among other things, I told him I wasn't going to sit in the car half the night waiting for him to come out of a party and then drive all the way back to Bicester! That's why."

"Oh, that."

"Yes, that!"

We could just see Harry in the distance, pelting down the quiet street which had council houses on one side and old people's bungalows on the other.

"Where's he going?" Dad muttered as we followed. About a hundred metres on, just after a bus stop, we caught up, and Dad told him to get in the car. Harry shook his head, panting. "Get in!" Dad repeated, but Harry just started walking off again.

Something broke inside me then. I felt so, so angry with Harry, and I'd had enough. I'd had to leave my football game at a crucial time. Megan was injured and Holly couldn't kick far and Amy was wearing silly boots and poor Daisy was marking Billy Whizz … and why? Because of *him*! My dumb, selfish, miserable brother!

I unbuckled my seatbelt and told Dad to stop the car. Then I jumped out, even though I only had socks on my feet, and started chasing Harry.

"What's the matter with you, Harry?" I yelled. "Why are you being so foul?"

He stopped abruptly, turned and folded his arms. "So I'm foul! Big deal!" he said, oh-so cockily.

"It *is* a big deal!" I shouted at the top of my voice, shoving at his arms so that he almost lost his balance and ended up in the hedge behind him. "It's a big deal to me, because you're making me hate you and I shouldn't hate you! I should *like* you, like Eve likes *her* big brothers!" I shoved him again. "And you should like me! And you should look out for me! But you don't! You just make fun of me, and it's not fair because I need you to look out for me more than ever now Mum and Dad have split up!" Tears were making my eyes blurry, so I could see not one but about six Harry heads. They all had surprised expressions on their faces.

"Need me? What do you need *me* for? As long as you've got your football or netball or tennis or some other crummy sport, that's all *you're* bothered about."

I gawped at him. "Are you serious? Even if I played for England in ten different teams and in ten different sports, it wouldn't be the same as having a big brother on my side!"

"Whatever," Harry said, but his voice didn't sound quite as sneery.

A woman pushing her baby in a buggy said "Excuse me" and sidled past. I swallowed and turned back towards the car. Dad was standing there, looking sadder than I'd seen him in a long time. "I want to go home," I told him.

"We can't…" he began.

"We can!" I said. "I don't want to spend the day traipsing around Mowborough or in the car driving to Bicester with *him*. I want to go home."

"Lucy, it's different now…"

I felt sharp tears spring up again. "I don't care!"

"Lucy, love…"

"No! You and Mum promised that our lives wouldn't change that much when you split up, but they have! Loads! Harry was never this horrid before. You were never this tired. Mum was never this bossy and I was never this … this … muddled up." I turned back to Harry. "That's why I like football. Hannah says 'Mark number 7 or 8 or whatever' so I mark number 7 or 8. I don't have to write a list to remember a thousand things about it. I just mark. I can handle that. I can't handle this."

Harry nodded. "I know," he said quietly.

I turned back to Dad. "I want to go home," I repeated.

Reluctantly, Dad called Mum on his mobile, telling her how upset I was, so she agreed to let us come back. I nodded and slid into the back of the car.

By the time we got home I had stopped crying but I still felt wound up.

At first, when she saw I had calmed down, Mum was really cross, accusing Dad of giving in to us and ganging up on her. "It's two days out of seven!" she ranted, pacing up and down the living-room floor. "And I'm not exactly living the party lifestyle during those two days either, you know." Her hands fluttered over the pile of ironing she'd been doing.

"You *always* say that, Mum!" I told her. "But it's two of the best days. The days when we're supposed to chill out."

"So chill out! I'm not stopping you! How you all spend the weekend is up to you. But you'll forgive me for needing a break too, won't you? Or am I not allowed one?"

There was a long pause. Dad glared at the carpet, his jaw doing its clenching thing. Harry mumbled, "I knew she'd be like this." And I said, "No."

"Pardon me?" Mum asked in her most fearsome PE teacher's voice.

I looked her in the eye, remembering what Eve's mum had told me about being a single parent. "No," I said, more loudly this time, "you don't get a break. Neither does Dad. When you have kids that's it. Twenty-four-seven. You're stuck with us. Sorry if you don't want us. I don't want Amy Minter on our football team, either, but I'm stuck with her. That's life."

Mum's eyes watered. "Of course I want you! I love you both very much. It's just having the weekend free lets me recharge my batteries."

I took a deep breath. I needed to explain properly. "I know! I get it! I'm not saying you have to look after us at weekends *instead* of Dad. I'm just saying we need to be able to come home sometimes. I hate … I hate having to wear my footy shorts underneath my jeans all day because I can't get changed properly. I hate eating out all the time. I hate Harry hating watching me play football – it puts me off…"

"And I hate missing out on stuff all my mates are doing," Harry mumbled, coming to stand next to me. "Nobody in my year spends *all* Saturday and *all* Sunday with their dad, except the freaks. No offence, Dad – you're cool, but, you know…"

"I know, I know," Dad replied.

"And, Mum, I admit I've been giving you a hard time lately, but you just don't listen … like the other night…" Harry continued.

It was as if we'd both turned on a tap and

couldn't turn it off again. Poor Mum's eyes got wider and wider, until she slumped down in the armchair opposite Dad. "And there's us thinking dividing the week up like this seemed the simplest way!"

Dad nodded. He seemed too dazed to speak.

"But it's not, is it?" Mum sighed. She turned to us. "Harry, Lucy, go and make us a pot of tea, will you? I want to talk to your dad alone for a few minutes."

Harry and me must have been the slowest tea-makers ever. We waited ages and ages before we even put the kettle on to boil, with me going to the kitchen door every two minutes to listen to how their voices sounded. "They're talking so fast!" I whispered to Harry.

"At least they're talking and not blowing a fuse."

"Yeah," I said, "not like some people I could mention."

He blushed. My big brother, Harry, actually blushed! "Soz. Didn't mean to be such a wally earlier … you know … at the match."

"S'OK. Just don't do it again."

"Or else?" He grinned.

"I'll set Jenny-Jane Bayliss on you."

"The bolshy one?" (So he *had* noticed someone on the pitch!)

"Yep."

"I hear you."

A few seconds later Mum stuck her head round the door. "Lucy, where's your fixture list?" she asked.

"On the pinboard in my bedroom," I said, and she disappeared again.

Then Dad stuck his head round the door. "I thought you two were making a pot of tea?"

"We are," I said.

"Get on with it, then. I'm parched."

Harry carried the pot in on a tray and I brought biscuits – chocolate fingers arranged like sun rays, with a jammy dodger in the middle.

"Right," said Mum, my fixture list in her lap, "we've worked out a solution."

"We hope," said Dad, slurping his tea. He had a huge grin on his face and for one tiny, tiny, tiny second I thought he might be going to say that he was coming back to live with us again – but Mum soon squashed that idea.

"Not every weekend, but *some* weekends ... especially those where you have a Sunday fixture, Lucy, I'm going to go away for the weekend."

"Where?" I asked, anxious now that she might be upset and leave us for ever.

"Oh, I don't know. A nice spa somewhere with friends from the department ... Auntie Laura's in Leeds, maybe ... London ... Edinburgh. Wherever I fancy! It'll be nice to have a complete break."

"Oh," I said. "OK."

"And I get to stay here," Dad said, dunking two chocolate fingers into his cup.

My heart leapt at that! "What? You'll sleep over?"

"Uh-huh."

"So we can watch *Gillette Soccer Saturday* together?"

"Uh-huh."

"And I get a lie-in?" Harry asked.

"Uh-huh."

"And we can have mates round?"

"Uh-huh."

"Sorted!" we said together. I turned and high-fived Harry. He high-fived me back with such a clout it stung like mad, but I didn't mind. In that instant all the bad atmosphere that had been swirling round over the past few weeks just vanished.

"I'm going to get changed," I said, "and then I'm going to phone Megan and find out what the score was."

"And then the three of us will go out to Pasta Roma," Dad said, "and leave your mum to the ironing."

"Thanks a bunch." Mum grinned.

"Unless you want to join us?"

"I just might," she said.

Final Whistle

I am gutted to report we lost to the Tembridge Vixens four—two in the end. They equalized just before half-time, and in the second half that Ninja scored a hat-trick, with Gemma pulling one back a minute before the final whistle. Holly was given Parsnip of the Match, though, because apparently she was wicked in goal — the Vixens could easily have netted six or seven if she hadn't pulled off some mighty saves by punching the ball out left, right and centre. "She could take up boxing, no fear," Megan said, laughing.

Nobody mentioned the incident with Harry, but Eve told me that if I ever needed to talk about brothers or cheesy feet (she said they were the same thing), she'd be there for me. That's a true team-mate for you.

Luckily Harry's been amazing since the new weekend arrangements started. He even comes to watch me play sometimes … without being bribed. Miracles do happen.

Dad's happier, too. He told me the highlight of his week is watching Gillette Soccer Saturday with his favourite daughter, then watching Hot Fuzz with his favourite son, while sitting in his favourite chair. He can google away without Mum breathing down his neck, too. Oh! That reminds me. Nettie Honeyball. It turns out Nettie is a legend in women's footballing history. She was one of the first women ever to get a ladies' football team together. It was called the British Ladies' Football Club and was based in London and founded in 1895. Yes, 1895! In your face, boys who think girls began playing in 2001 or something. Eat Nettie's shorts!

Daisy and Dylan McNeil are going to continue the story of our first season. They're going to concentrate on the cup run. That should be good! Knowing Dylan and Daisy, it will be upside-down or written in Elvish or something. Good luck!

Truly yours,
Lucy Skidmore xxx

More from Girls F.C.

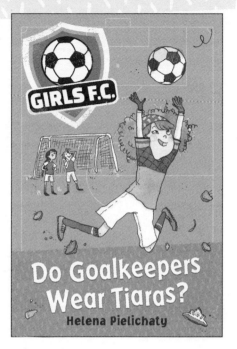

Megan is desperate to be picked for her
school football team. She tries everything
to get the coach to notice her (even wearing
a tiara) but nothing seems to work. That's
when she has her big idea: she could start
her own team. An all-girls team!

Now she just needs a pitch, a coach — oh,
and at least ten other players…

More from Girls F.C.

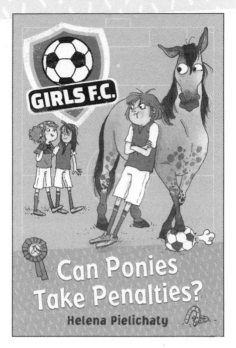

Petra can't wait to play in her first football tournament. While she's not exactly the best defender, it's great spending time with her friend Megan — the team captain.

But the big match clashes with her sister's show-jumping event and, as usual, Charlotte (and her dumb ponies) are her mum's number one priority...

More from Girls F.C.

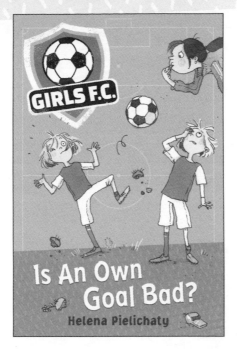

Twins Daisy and Dylan adore playing
football, but they never make it to practice
on time and their antics on and off the pitch
are beginning to annoy their teammates.

When Megan, the captain, tells the twins
she is unhappy with their match-reports they
ask their Scottish granny for help. Luckily,
she knows just how to turn things around...